THE DINOSAUR THAT POOPED THE BED!

Check out Danny and Dinosaur in more adventures:

THE DINOSAUR THAT POOPED CHRISTMAS
THE DINOSAUR THAT POOPED A PLANET!
THE DINOSAUR THAT POOPED THE PAST!
THE DINOSAUR THAT POOPED SPACE: STICKER ACTIVITY BOOK
THE DINOSAUR THAT POOPED A PLANET! SOUND BOOK
THE DINOSAUR THAT POOPED A LOT!

For Buzz, who poops more than Dino - T.F.
I would like to dedicate this book to the twinkle in my eye - D.P.
For Codie & Kyle - G.P.

THE DINOSAUR THAT POOPED THE BED!
A RED FOX BOOK 978 1 782 95179 7
Published in Great Britain by Red Fox,
an imprint of Random House Children's Publishers UK
A Penguin Random House Company

Penguin Random House UK

This edition published 2015
Simultaneously published in hardback by Hutchinson

3 5 7 9 10 8 6 4

Illustrated by Garry Parsons

Red Fox Books are published by Random House Children's Publishers UK,
61–63 Uxbridge Road, London, W5 5SA

www.**randomhousechildrens**.co.uk
www.**randomhouse**.co.uk
www.**totallyrandombooks**.co.uk

Addresses for companies within The Random House Group Limited can be found at:
www.randomhouse.co.uk/offices.htm
THE RANDOM HOUSE GROUP Limited Reg. No. 954009
A CIP catalogue record for this book is available from the British Library.

Printed in China

THE DINOSAUR THAT POOPED THE BED!

Tom Fletcher and Dougie Poynter
Illustrated by Garry Parsons

RED FOX

Danny and Dino had nothing to do,
So Danny said, "Why don't we watch some cartoons!"
But then Danny's mum cast a shadow of gloom.
"You can't watch TV till you've tidied your room."

They slumped up the stairs in the foulest of grumps
And stood in their room at the foot of Mount Dump.
"Tidying this mess will take thousands of years,"
Said Danny whilst desperately holding back tears.

Unless they were going to tidy for ever,
They needed a plan – a plan that was clever.

And then an idea popped inside Danny's head.
"Why clean up this mess? You can eat it instead!"

So Dinosaur opened its mouth like a bin:
Dan scooped up the mess and he threw it all in.

Toys from the tip of the top of the heap
Were chucked in and chomped by the dinosaur's teeth.

It chewed Danny's shoes, it could not get enough
Of teddies and cuddly stuff made of fluff.
The dinosaur sucked like a humungous hoover,
Removing the mess like a room-mess remover.

Vests, pants and socks and little toy soldiers . . .
Dan laughed as he watched from the dinosaur's shoulders.
His fluffy pet hamster, along with its cage,
Was swallowed in Dinosaur's mess-munching rage.

It smushed the CDs, which, on reflection,
Were far from the greatest of record collections.
So Dan didn't mind – it all had to go
If they wanted to kick back and watch TV shows . . .

In Dinosaur's head the bed was a burger,
As diamonds would look to the greediest burglar.
In one dino-bite the bed disappeared –
No mess left in sight, the whole room had been cleared.

Not one piece of rubbish was left to consume –
"At last we can finally watch some cartoons!"
But Dinosaur's tum cast a shadow of doom:
It was full to the brim with the mess of Dan's room!

Dino was wedged in between floor and ceiling –
It couldn't believe how full up it was feeling.

It started to worry, it started to panic:
Never before had it been more gigantic!

The dinosaur's bottom was bigger than Norway,
So big and so fat it was blocking the doorway!

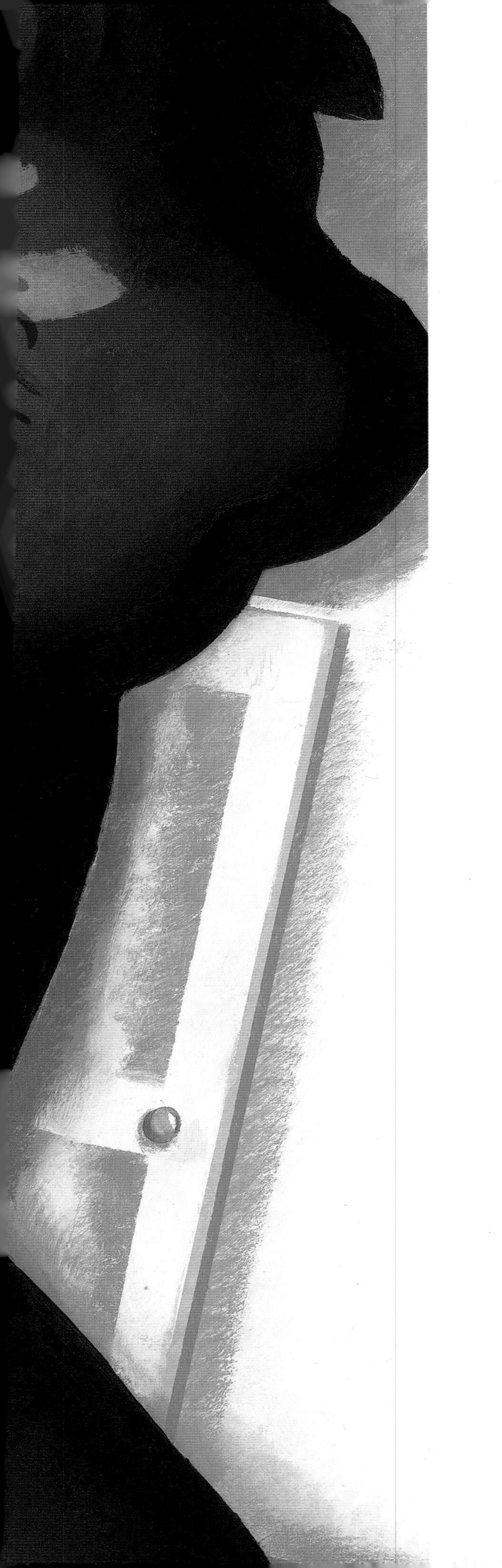

Then Dan started crying,

His nose dripped with snot –

They were stuck in their room
and the TV was not!

With pillows and quilts in the dinosaur's gut,
Its brain didn't have full control of its butt!

It knew that there wasn't a thing it could do:

One way or another,
it needed to . . .

POO!

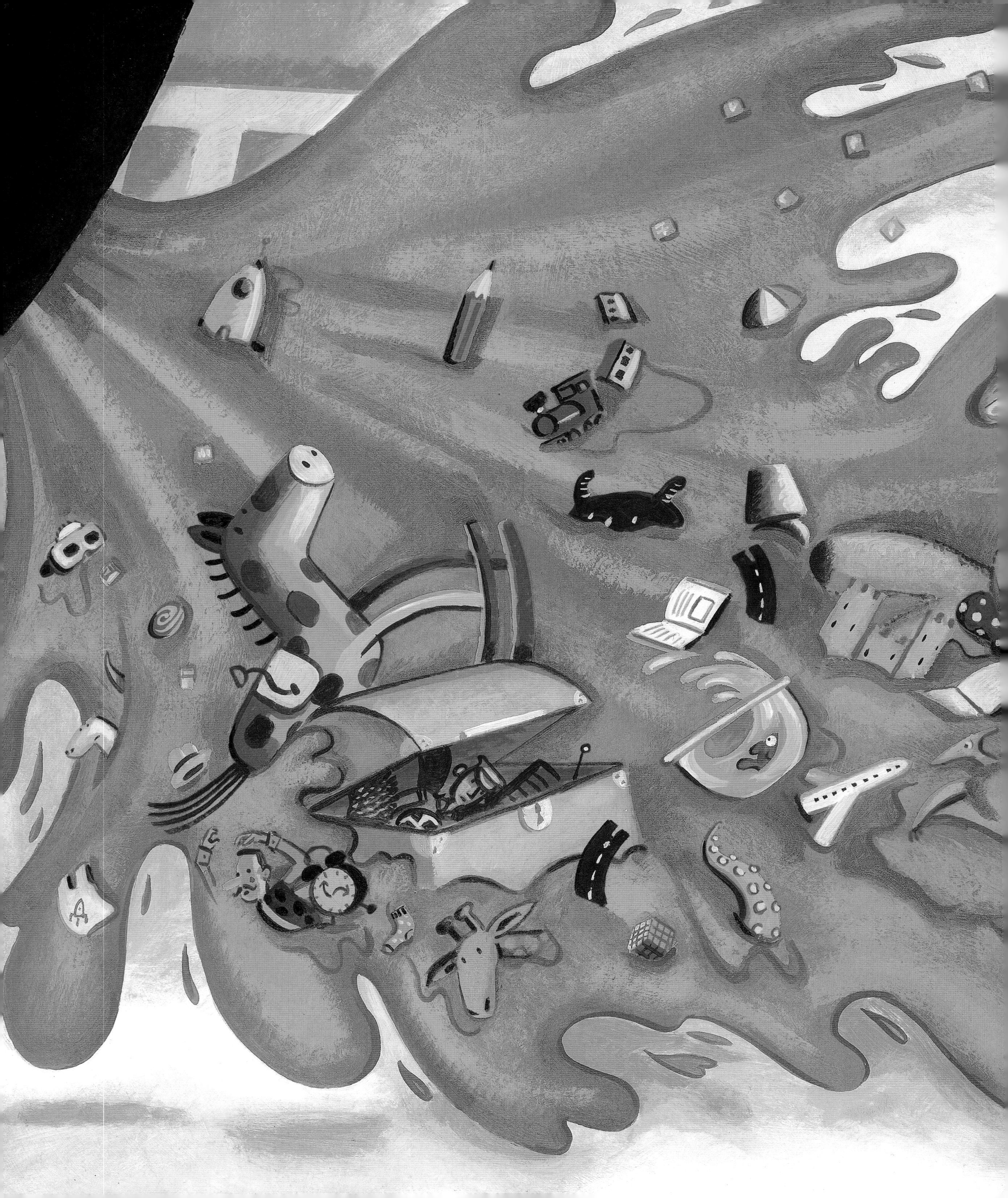

The dinosaur pooped more than ever before –
All the mess they had cleared was now back on the floor.
Shoes, pants and teddies, and soldiers and socks,
With smelly poo lumps filling Danny's toy box.

Then Danny saw Dinosaur's face turning red
And knew the next thing to be pooped was his bed.
It sprang from its bum with a bounce and a bump
Right back to its place at the base of Mount Dump.

Then Dino deflated and unblocked the door,
Where Mummy was standing, more cross than before.
They looked at the mess all around where they stood
And knew they'd been naughty, and naughty's not good.

So they picked up their mops and mopped up the plops
That covered the toys and the vests, pants and socks.

If only they'd tidied their room as they should,
They'd be watching TV, not wishing they could.

So remember, next time you're in front of the telly:
You can't watch cartoons if your bedroom is smelly!